The Worst Kid
Who Ever Lived
on Eighth Avenue

The Worst Kid Who Ever Lived on Eighth Avenue

by Laurie Lawlor

illustrated by Cynthia Fisher

Holiday House/New York

For John James Lawlor,
Chicago fireman for 31 years
L. L.

For my sisters,
Christine and Susan
C. F.

Text copyright © 1998 by Laurie Lawlor
Illustrations copyright © 1998 by Cynthia Fisher
ALL RIGHTS RESERVED
Printed in the United States of America
FIRST EDITION
R.L. 2.6

Library of Congress Cataloging-in-Publication Data
Lawlor, Laurie.
The worst kid who ever lived on Eighth Avenue / by Laurie Lawlor;
illustrated by Cynthia Fisher.
p.   cm.
Summary: Trying to be detectives, Mary Lou and her friends imagine
that terrible crimes are being committed when Leroy, the worst kid
who ever lived on Eighth Avenue, returns to the house next door.
ISBN 0-8234-1350-0 (hardcover)
[1. Mystery and detective stories.   2. Neighbors—Fiction.]
I. Fisher, Cynthia, ill.   II. Title.
PZ7.L4189Wo   1998   97-28185   CIP   AC
[E]—dc21

Contents

1. *Special Delivery*

"How fast can you run?"

Leo asked Mary Lou.

Mary Lou bit her lip.

The mailbox
of the spooky house
next door looked very far away.
"Are you sure the Jukes are
on vacation?" Lynn asked.
Mary Lou nodded.
"I have to pick up
their mail every day."
"What about Gasher?" Leo asked.
Mary Lou looked at the windows.
She looked for
the big wolf dog.
"Gasher went to the kennel."
"What if Leroy comes back?"
Lynn said.
Leo whistled.
"The worst kid who
ever lived on Eighth Avenue."

"Everybody knows Leroy is bad news,"
Lynn said. "He set
Mrs. Prouty's tree on fire."
Mary Lou frowned.
"Leroy is grown up now.
He is probably in the army."
Leo shook his head.
"I heard he is in jail.
Of course,
he could always escape."
"I feel sick," Mary Lou said.

9

"Boo!"

Mary Lou jumped.

"Scared you!" shouted Tommy.

Mary Lou gave her younger

brother a nasty look.

"Mary Lou is afraid to pick up
  the Jukes' mail," Leo said.
"Well, *I* am not afraid,"
  Tommy said.
  He leapt up the porch steps.
  He grabbed the mail
  and ran back.
"Special delivery,"
  Tommy said and smiled.

2. *Just Like Real Detectives*

Later that morning,

Mary Lou, Leo, Lynn, and Tommy

climbed the tree

behind the garage.

They climbed on to the roof.

"Your garage,"

Leo said to Mary Lou,

"is the perfect place to watch

what's happening on Eighth Avenue."

Leo looked

through his binoculars.

"See anything exciting?"

Lynn asked.

Leo shook his head.

Lynn rolled her eyes.

"Nothing exciting ever

happens on Eighth Avenue."

Suddenly, there was a
terrific roar.

It was a car with sharp fins.
It screeched to a stop
in the Jukes' driveway.
"Who is that?" Lynn asked.
"Leroy!" Leo cried.
Tommy took the binoculars.
"What is he doing?"
Mary Lou whispered.

"He is taking something
  out of his trunk.
  Something big and bulky," Tommy said.
"Probably stolen money," Leo said.
"Let's help the police find clues.
  Then we'll get a reward.
  We'll be rich and famous."
  Tommy licked his lips.
"Then I could buy
  lots of candy."
"I'll be on TV," Lynn said.
"This is the most exciting thing
  that's ever happened on Eighth Avenue."

Leo smiled.

"I have a plan.

We'll stay up all night.

We'll watch the Jukes' house.

Maybe we'll see something."

"Just like real detectives!"

Tommy exclaimed.

"I hope when the police come

they blast their sirens."

3. *Scritch-Scratch*

Mary Lou and Lynn set up
the tent in the backyard.
Leo got the sleeping bags.
Tommy got the snacks.
Then the four detectives
took turns staring
at the house next door.

It was dark.

They waited and watched.

But nothing happened.

"This is not very exciting,"
Lynn said.

"Anyone want something to eat?"
Tommy said.

Mary Lou shined the flashlight.

"Those marshmallows look dirty,"
she said.

"But they still taste good,"
Tommy answered.

After a while, everyone fell asleep.

Scritch-scratch-scritch-scratch.

"Wake up!" Mary Lou whispered.

"I hear someone digging."

"Leroy's burying the money,"
Leo said.

"I'll sneak closer
and take a look,"
Tommy said.

When he came back,
he was out of breath.
"He's burying something big."
"*Billions* of dollars, I bet,"
Leo said.
"I think we should tell my mother.
She can call the police,"
Mary Lou said.
"Then will she get the reward?"
Lynn asked.

But Mary Lou's mother
did not believe their story.
"It is very late," she said.
"Go back to sleep."
"Can we bring
our sleeping bags inside?"
Mary Lou asked.
"All right," her mother answered.
"You have done enough
detective work for one night."

4.   *Clues!*

The next morning, Leroy's car
with the sharp fins was gone.
Leo looked in the driveway
for skid marks.
He looked on the sidewalk
for footprints.

Lynn looked at the Jukes' backyard
with the binoculars.
"Gasher dug up a lot of dirt piles.
  We'll never find the buried money."
"Maybe somebody should
  look on the front porch,"
Tommy said.

"That's *my* job," Mary Lou said.

She marched up the porch steps,

just like a real detective.

She noticed something important!

The window was open a crack.

Mary Lou waved to Lynn, Leo,

and Tommy.

She wanted them to see her.

She would do something brave,

something even Tommy would not try.

She opened the window wide.

She climbed inside.

24

"Come back!" Lynn called.

Her voice sounded very far away.

Mary Lou looked

around the living room.

It was messy.

But not very spooky.

She looked for clues.

She found dog biscuits, dog food,

dog toys, dog fur, dog smells.

But no clues.

What if Leroy came back?

She had to hurry.

She ran into the kitchen.

On the table she found some things.

One leather glove,

a long rope,

and a bunch of little flags.

Clues!

Over her head, she heard a loud

clunk!

She jumped.

Was someone upstairs?

She ran to the window.

She climbed out on to the porch.

She did not see

her friends waiting on the sidewalk.

She saw her mother.

And she looked very angry.

5.   Trapped

"You must never go
inside someone's house
without being asked,"
her mother said.
She sent Mary Lou to her room.

Mary Lou had to think about
what she'd done.
She could not watch television.
She could not play with anyone,
not even Tommy.
Mary Lou drew pictures.
She drew the things
from the Jukes' house.

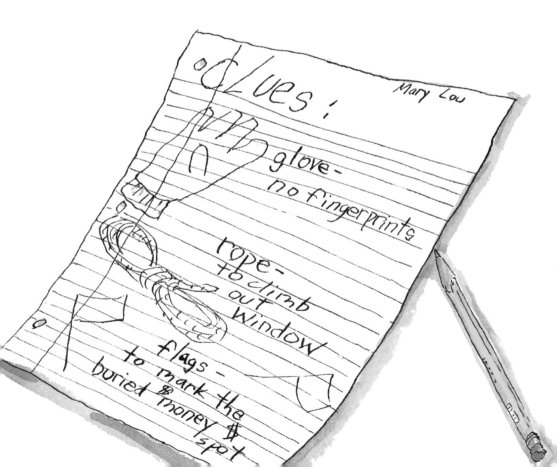

"Now I know what the clues mean!"
she said.

Mary Lou frowned.

What if Leroy left town?

No one would ever find out

who stole the money.

She and her friends

would never get a reward.

She had to tell the police

about the clues.

But how could she?

She wasn't supposed to

leave her bedroom.

Mary Lou had an idea.

She opened the window.

Lynn, Leo, and Tommy

were standing below.

"Hey!" Mary Lou shouted.
She made her picture of the clues
into a paper airplane.
Then she sent it flying.
Tommy unfolded the paper.
He and the others
looked at her drawing.

Then the three detectives ran away.

Mary Lou did a happy detective dance.

Leo, Lynn, and Tommy were

on their way to the police station.

They had her list of clues.

Any minute a police car

would speed down Eighth Avenue.

Its sirens would be shrieking.

Mary Lou waited.

Nothing happened.

Knock! Knock-knock-a-knock!

"Who's there?" she said.

"Special delivery!" Tommy whispered.

"Here is everything you wanted

for your escape.

I've got to go.

Mom might catch me.

Good luck!"

The door slammed shut.

Mary Lou sighed.

Solving crimes was hard work.

6. A Surprise Visit

Finally, Mary Lou was allowed
to see her friends again.
She told them about the clues.
"We're too late,"
Leo said. "Leroy is gone."
"He could be at
the arctic circle by now,"
Lynn said.
Tommy patted Mary Lou.
"Don't feel so bad," he said.
"You were brave to go
inside the Jukes' house."
Suddenly, they saw a gleaming car.
It had a siren on the roof.
It roared into
the driveway next door.

"Is the Jukes' house burning?"
Leo asked.

Mary Lou sniffed.

"I don't smell any smoke."

"Who called the fire marshall?"
Lynn said.

"Let's go see," Leo said.

The four friends
crossed the yard.

They peeked around a bush.

A fire marshall in a big hat
got out of the car.
He wore shiny shoes.
He carried flowers.
"Did you forget the hose?"
Tommy asked.
"Where's the hook
and ladder truck?"

Mary Lou elbowed him hard.

"Shhhh!"

The fire marshall
turned to the children.

"There's no fire," he said.

"Leroy!" Leo cried.

Mary Lou, Lynn, and Tommy froze.
This was the closest
any of them had ever
been to Leroy Jukes,
the worst kid who
ever lived on Eighth Avenue.
They didn't move.
Something frisky jumped
out of the backseat.

"Come, Juno,"
Leroy called to the puppy.
It sniffed everyone's shoes.
"Let's get ready
for your tracking lessons."

"Tracking?" Tommy asked.

"This is a special dog,"
   Leroy explained.

"I'm training him to help me.
   He will use his nose
   to find out where and how
   a fire starts."

"But you said there
   wasn't any fire here,"
   Leo said.

"I'm just showing Juno around,"
   Leroy said.

"My parents will keep him
   while I am out of town."

"Are you *really* a fire marshall?"
   Tommy asked.

"Yes, I am," Leroy said and laughed.

"How do you train a tracking dog?"

Mary Lou asked.

She was not convinced.

"First, I set up a course for Juno.

I use flags," Leroy said.

"Then Juno looks for a hidden glove.

42

I tie a long rope on him.

When he finds the glove,

he gets a treat."

"Oh," said Mary Lou.

Now she understood.

The glove, rope, and flags

were for training Juno.

"Why do you need flowers?" Lynn asked.

"These are for old Gasher's grave,"

Leroy said.

He looked very sad.

"Gasher got sick

and died at the kennel.

I had to bury him

the other night in the yard.

He was such a good dog.

I miss him already."

Leroy looked like he might cry.

Mary Lou felt sad, too.

Then Juno jumped and barked.

He ran around the children.

"Juno needs to get used to

many different people.

Then he will be a calm tracking dog,"
Leroy said.

He looked at Mary Lou.

"You did a good job with the mail.
Would you like to help walk Juno
while I'm gone?"

"Sure!" said Mary Lou.
She felt proud.
"Thank you," Leroy said.
He picked up Juno
and went inside.

Tommy watched
the back door slam shut.
"I guess Leroy isn't so bad,"
he said slowly.
And the four friends climbed
on to the garage roof.
They waited to see
what exciting thing
would happen next
on Eighth Avenue.